LIGHTNING BOLT BOOKS™

Meet a Baby Wallaby

Anna Leigh

Lerner Publications • Minneapolis

For Emmie

Lerner Publications Company
A division of Lerner Publishing Group, Inc.
241 First Avenue North
Minneapolis, MN 55401 USA

For reading levels and more information, look up this title at www.lernerbooks.com.

Library of Congress Cataloging-in-Publication Data

Names: Leigh, Anna, author.
Title: Meet a baby wallaby / Anna Leigh.
Description: Minneapolis : Lerner Publications, [2017] | Series: Lightning bolt books. Baby Australian animals | Audience: Ages 6-9. | Audience: K to grade 3. | Includes bibliographical references and index.
Identifiers: LCCN 2016038348 (print) | LCCN 2016052448 (ebook) | ISBN 9781512433869 (lb : alk. paper) | ISBN 9781512450583 (eb pdf)
Subjects: LCSH: Wallabies—Infancy—Juvenile literature. | Wallabies—Life cycles—Juvenile literature.
Classification: LCC QL737.M35 L4445 2017 (print) | LCC QL737.M35 (ebook) | DDC 599.2/2139—dc23

LC record available at https://lccn.loc.gov/2016038348

Manufactured in the United States of America
1-42022-23892-10/20/2016

Table of Contents

A Tiny Baby

This red-necked wallaby is about to give birth! Her baby has been growing inside her for about thirty days.

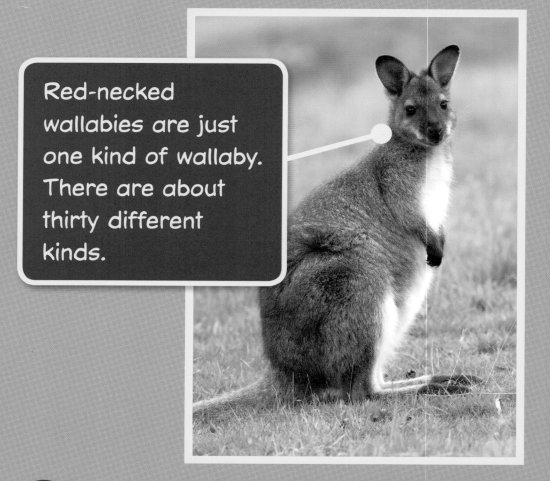

Red-necked wallabies are just one kind of wallaby. There are about thirty different kinds.

Wallabies are closely related to kangaroos. Kangaroos and wallabies look similar, but wallabies are usually smaller.

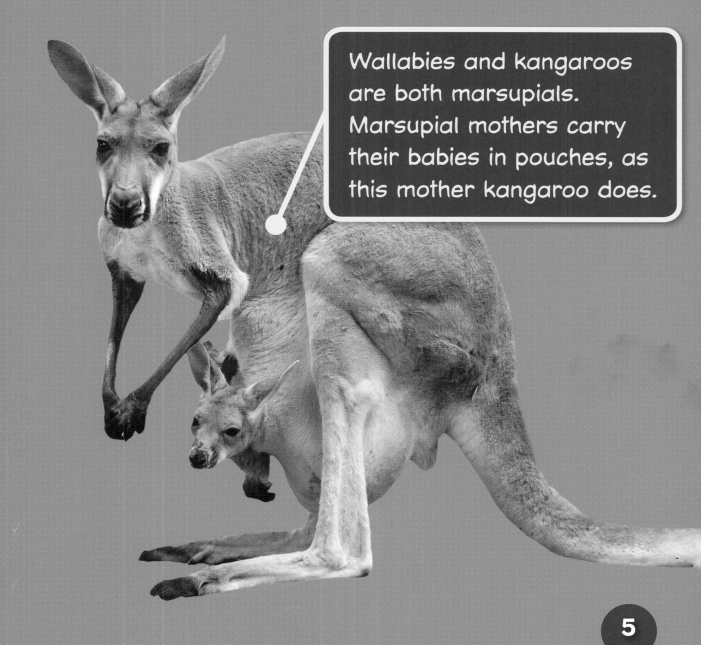

Wallabies and kangaroos are both marsupials. Marsupial mothers carry their babies in pouches, as this mother kangaroo does.

A baby wallaby is called a joey. A newborn joey is very tiny. It doesn't have fur, and it can't see or hear.

This is a baby tammar wallaby. A baby wallaby weighs less than 0.04 ounces (1 gram). It is about the size of a grape!

The joey must climb into its mother's pouch right after it is born. It will finish growing there. The joey stays in the pouch for the next several months.

Staying Safe

When the joey is about five months old, it starts to poke its head out from the pouch to look around. It leaves the pouch for the first time one month later.

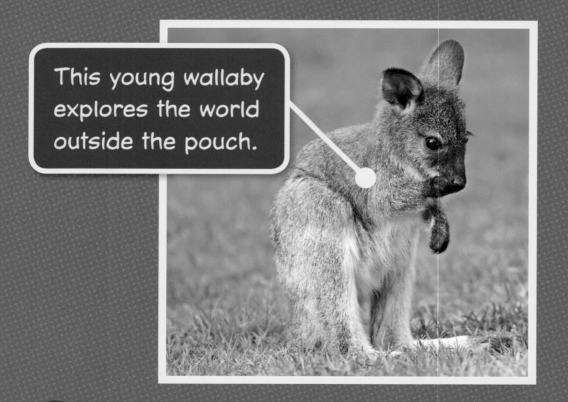

This young wallaby explores the world outside the pouch.

The joey stays close to its mother. Dingoes and eagles are some predators of wallabies. The joey will jump back into the pouch as soon as it senses danger.

A predator is an animal that hunts and eats other animals.

Wallabies often spend time alone. But they may feed in groups of up to thirty wallabies. The group is known as a mob.

This wallaby eats in a group.

When it is eight months old, the joey leaves its mother's pouch for good. But the joey is not finished growing. It will stay close to its mother for a few more months.

Finding Food

Joeys drink milk from their mothers. For the first four months, the joey is always attached to a teat in the pouch.

A joey continues to drink milk until it is about one year old.

A joey that has left the pouch eats grass, shrubs, and berries along with drinking its mother's milk. Wallabies also dig up roots to eat. These roots give wallabies water.

Wallabies have sharp claws for digging.

13

Wallabies use their molars to grind down the tough plants they eat. Over time, the molars move forward in their mouths. Then they fall out. A wallaby will go through four pairs of molars in its lifetime.

Molars are large teeth near the back of the jaw.

Wallabies usually spend the day in sheltered, wooded areas or near caves. They go out into open areas at night to search for food.

This wallaby scans an open area for food.

Living on Their Own

A female wallaby is ready to have joeys of her own when she is about fourteen months old. Male wallabies are not fully developed until they are nineteen months old.

This wallaby is fully grown.

A fully grown male wallaby weighs about 44 pounds (20 kilograms). Females weigh only about 26 pounds (12 kg). Both have strong legs and tails that are almost as long as the rest of their bodies.

Wallabies are active at night and rest during the day. But they are always alert for danger. Wallabies have excellent hearing to help them sense when danger is near.

A wallaby's long ears can turn forward and backward to listen for predators.

Male and female wallabies both live for about fifteen years. Baby wallabies continue to be born, so the wallaby life cycle goes on.

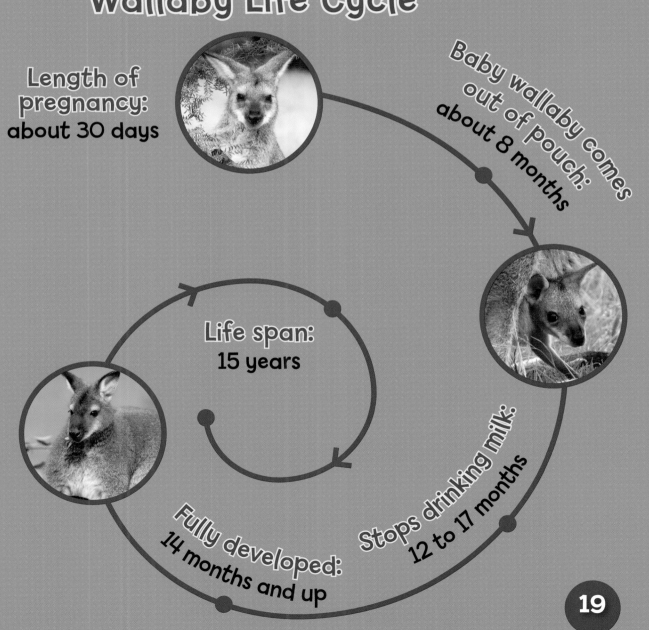

Wallaby Life Cycle

Length of pregnancy: about 30 days

Baby wallaby comes out of pouch: about 8 months

Life span: 15 years

Stops drinking milk: 12 to 17 months

Fully developed: 14 months and up

Habitat in Focus

- Red-necked wallabies live on mainland Australia as well as on Tasmania. Wallabies in mainland Australia give birth to joeys all year long. But in Tasmania, most joeys are born in February and March.

- Australia is often very dry and hot. But wallabies don't need to drink much water. They can get water from the plants they eat.

- Eucalypt forests are common in Australia. Red-necked wallabies live in these forests. These trees give them shelter from the hot sun during the day.

Fun Facts

- Red-necked wallabies are named for the red color of the fur on their shoulders. The rest of their fur is gray or white.

- Red-necked wallabies lick their arms to keep cool.

- Wallabies have small vocal cords. Sometimes they have no vocal cords. This means they can't make much sound. Instead, wallabies stamp their feet to warn one another of danger.

- Wallabies use their long tails for balance while they are hopping.

Glossary

alert: careful, watchful, and ready to act

dingo: a wild dog that lives in Australia

molar: a large tooth near the back of the jaw used for grinding food

predator: an animal that lives by killing and eating other animals

related: belonging to the same group because of similar characteristics

teat: the part of a female animal through which a young animal drinks milk

Further Reading

BioExpedition: Wallaby
http://www.bioexpedition.com/wallaby

Easy Science for Kids: Marsupials
http://easyscienceforkids.com/animals/mammals
/marsupials

Kalman, Bobbie. *Baby Marsupials*. New York:
Crabtree, 2012.

Kidcyber: Wallabies
http://www.kidcyber.com.au/wallabies

Leigh, Anna. *Meet a Baby Kangaroo*. Minneapolis:
Lerner Publications, 2018.

Index

Photo Acknowledgments

The images in this book are used with the permission of: © Joel Sartore/Getty Images, pp. 2, 23; © Steven David Miller/NPL/Minden Pictures, p. 4; © Anankkml/Dreamstime.com, p. 5; © D. Parer and E. Parer-Cook/Minden Pictures, p. 6; © John Cancalosi/Alamy, p. 7; © Christian Hütter/imageBROKER/Alamy, p. 8; © Sheralee Stoll/Alamy, p. 9; © Alexpolo/ Dreamstime.com, p. 10; © blickwinkel/DuM Sheldon/Alamy, p. 11; © Steve Lovegrove/ Dreamstime.com, p. 12; © Holger Ehlers/Alamy, p. 13; © Kevin Howchin/Alamy, p. 14; © Marc Anderson/Alamy, p. 15; © Ingo Schulz/imageBROKER/Alamy, p. 16; © Dave King/ Getty Images, p. 17; © Stephanie Jackson/Australian wildlife collection/Alamy, p. 18; © B. G. Thomson/Science Source, p. 19 (top); © Martin Willis/Minden Pictures, p. 19 (right); © Corbis/VCG/Getty Images, p. 19 (left).

Front cover: © Dave Watts/Minden Pictures.

Main body text set in Billy Infant regular 28/36. Typeface provided by SparkType.